Phonics Friends

Yoshi's Yard
The Sound of Y

By Joanne Meier and Cecilia Minden

The Child's World

Published in the United States of America
by The Child's World®
PO Box 326
Chanhassen, MN 55317-0326
800-599-READ
www.childsworld.com

A special thank you to Cheryl Sanks, Tanner "Yoshi" Sanks,
and Ben "York" Reichert for their superb modeling and to
Sue Melaniphy for making her yard available to us.

The Child's World®: Mary Berendes, Publishing Director

Editorial Directions, Inc.: E. Russell Primm, Editorial Director
and Project Editor; Katie Marsico, Associate Editor; Judith
Shiffer, Associate Editor and School Media Specialist;
Linda S. Koutris, Photo Researcher and Selector

The Design Lab: Kathleen Petelinsek, Design and Page
Production

Photographs ©: Photo setting and photography by Romie
and Alice Flanagan/Flanagan Publishing Services.

Library of Congress Cataloging-in-Publication Data
Meier, Joanne D.
  Yoshi's yard : the sound of Y / by Joanne Meier and
Cecilia Minden.
     p. cm. — (Phonics friends)
  Summary: Simple text featuring the sound of the letter "y"
describes Yoshi and his friend York playing.
  ISBN 1-59296-310-2 (library bound : alk. paper) [1.
English language—Phonetics. 2. Reading.] I. Minden,
Cecilia. II. Title. III. Series.
  PZ7.M5148Yo 2004
  [E]—dc22   2004003545

Note to parents and educators:
The Child's World® has created Phonics Friends with the goal of exposing children to engaging stories and pictures that assist in phonics development. The books in the series will help children learn the relationships between the letters of written language and the individual sounds of spoken language. This contact helps children learn to use these relationships to read and write words.

The books in this series follow a similar format. An introductory page, to be read by an adult, introduces the child to the phonics feature, or sound, that will be highlighted in the book. Read this page to the child, stressing the phonic feature. Help the student learn how to form the sound with her mouth. The Phonics Friends story and engaging photographs follow the introduction. At the end of the story, word lists categorize the feature words into their phonic element. Additional information on using these lists is on The Child's World® Web site listed at the top of this page.

Each book in this series has been carefully written to meet specific readability requirements. Close attention has been paid to elements such as word count, sentence length, and vocabulary. Readability formulas measure the ease with which the text can be read and understood. Each Phonics Friends book has been analyzed using the Spache readability formula. For more information on this formula, as well as the levels for each of the books in this series please visit The Child's World® Web site.

Reading research suggests that systematic phonics instruction can greatly improve students' word recognition, spelling, and comprehension skills. The Phonics Friends series assists in the teaching of phonics by providing students with important opportunities to apply their knowledge of phonics as they read words, sentences, and text.

Yoshi is playing in his yard.

It is a big yard!

Boys like to play in Yoshi's yard.

They can yell and run fast.

Yoshi's friend York comes to play. "What do you want to do today?" asks Yoshi.

"Yes, we're fine," says Yoshi.

"We're not done yet!"

Fun Facts

Yellow is a primary color. Red and blue are also primary colors. A primary color cannot be made from other colors. You can create other colors by mixing primary colors. You can make orange by mixing yellow and red. You can create green by mixing yellow and blue. During times of war, you might notice trees with yellow ribbons tied around them. These ribbons express hope that men and women who are serving in the war will return home safely.

You might think people yell only when they're angry, but this isn't always true. Before there were newspapers, town criers let everyone know what was going on in the world. These people read the news aloud throughout the town. They had to yell the information so people could hear what they had to say.

Activity

Creating Colors

Gather yellow, red, and blue paints. Put each color in its own bowl or cup. Mix a little yellow and a little red on a paper plate. See what color you get. Keep experimenting to see all the different shades of orange you can create using different amounts of yellow and red. Next try combining yellow and blue. Finally, paint a picture using all the different colors you have created.

To Learn More

Books
About the Sound of Y
Flanagan, Alice K. *Yum! The Sound of Y*. Chanhassen, Minn.: The Child's World.
  2000.

About Yards
Herman, Gail, and Jerry Smath (illustrator). *Buried in the Backyard*. New York:
  Kane Press, 2003.
Rockwell, Anne F., and Harlow Rockwell. *My Back Yard*. New York: Macmillan
  Publishing Co., 1984.

About Yelling
Eschbacher, Roger, and Adrian Johnson (illustrator). *Nonsense! He Yelled*.
  New York: Dial Books for Young Readers, 2002.
Sondheimer, Ilse, and Dee deRosa (illustrator). *The Boy Who Could Make
  His Mother Stop Yelling*. Fayetteville, N.Y.: Rainbow Press, 1982.

About Yellow
Ehlert, Lois. *Red Leaf, Yellow Leaf*. San Diego: Harcourt Brace Jovanovich, 1991.
Liu, Jae Soo. *Yellow Umbrella*. La Jolla, Calif.: Kane/Miller Book Publishers, 2002.

Web Sites
Visit our home page for lots of links about the Sound of Y:

http://www.childsworld.com/links.html

Note to Parents, Teachers, and Librarians: We routinely check our Web links to make
sure they're safe, active sites—so encourage your readers to check them out!

Y Feature Words

Proper Names

York

Yoshi

Feature Words in Initial Position

yard

yell

yelling

yellow

yes

yet

you

your

About the Authors

Joanne Meier, PhD, has worked as an elementary school teacher and university professor. She earned her BA in early childhood education from the University of South Carolina, and her MEd and PhD in education from the University of Virginia. She currently works as a literacy consultant for schools and private organizations. Joanne Meier lives with her husband Eric, and spends most of her time chasing her two daughters, Kella and Erin, and her two cats, Sam and Gilly, in Charlottesville, Virginia.

Cecilia Minden, PhD, directs the Language and Literacy Program at the Harvard Graduate School of Education. She is a reading specialist with classroom and administrative experience in grades K–12. She earned her PhD in reading education from the University of Virginia. Cecilia and her husband Dave Cupp enjoy sharing their love of reading with their granddaughter Chelsea.